MIMI AND HER DAD GO ON A SAFARI

Dr. Elizabeth Waiguchu Jackson

PICTURES BY
Christopher J. Jackson

For my husband Chris and the kids who worked alongside me to make writing and illustrating this book a wonderful journey.

Muthoni, an amazing girl.

For Mugure, a beautiful soul never forgotten.

FOREWORD

Dear reader,

As a mother of children who delight in nature, I am reminded each day that the world presents a festival of awe-inspiring animals. Sadly, I am also regularly reminded that man still has a long way to go in fully protecting our animals from harm and destruction. It is my hope that this book will help young people acquire and expand an appreciation for the wide variety of animals with which we share this planet and come to stand in awe of how beautifully they are created. I want these pages to impart my belief in the importance of preserving our wild animals and the natural environments that are necessary to support them. Our future generations deserve nothing less.

THE TRIP BEGINS

Mimi is a ten-year-old girl from North America with strong ties to Africa. Baba, Mimi's dad, promised to take Mimi on an African safari if she excelled in her schoolwork. She soon did just that, and her dad was eager to fulfill his promise. Baba had been on several safaris and was well versed in the geography and the wide variety of animals they would encounter on their trip. For as far back as Mimi could remember he had told wonderful stories about his encounters with elephants, zebras, tigers, and such. She could hardly wait to see them all for herself.

On the day before they set out on their long trip, Mimi and Baba packed their bags with pants, sneakers, hats, sunglasses, sweaters, shirts, and other necessities. Mimi considered taking her favorite red dress and red shoes but figured they would not be appropriate for a safari. She packed several of her favorite storybooks and a camera so she could take lots of photographs to show her friends when she returned. Both she and her dad had to choose carefully so their bags would not weigh more than the airline would allow.

The airport was huge and filled with strangers rushing this way and that. She held tightly to her dad's hand. He instructed Mimi to stay by his side and not talk to strangers.

As usual, she listened well. She followed him to the end of the long line which led to the ticket counter. They waited patiently as the line slowly moved along.

At last it was their turn to begin the check-in process. Baba presented their passports to the woman behind the counter and told her they had three bags. The woman looked back and forth between Mimi and her passport picture, eventually asking, "What is your name, young lady?"

Mimi whispered, "I am Mimi, and this is my dad."

The woman pushed her glasses down her nose and asked Baba where they were going. Baba explained that they were headed to Africa to go on safari. The lady smiled and said she had been on several safaris and had really enjoyed them. She wished them a good time and pointed them toward their next stop—the airport security checkpoint.

Her dad reminded Mimi to stick close to his side. That line was the longest and slowest-moving line Mimi had ever been in. Behind them was a man who complained that he was about to miss his flight because the line was not moving fast enough. The security agent explained that he had to follow the rules and procedures for everybody's comfort and safety.

During the check-in process another security agent announced that one of their bags would need to be opened. It was a routine part of the security check. Mimi was surprised they chose her red bag. She looked up at her dad and he smiled and nodded.

"Just part of the process," he said.

The bag held two of Mimi's favorite lotions. Lotion containers were not allowed on flights, so Baba was instructed to remove the bottles and place them in the huge trash bin behind them. Baba had told Mimi not to pack any liquids, but Mimi had not understood that lotion was really a liquid. She was sad because she had bought them with money she had been saving for a long time. She asked the agent if she could give the lotions to a homeless person instead of throwing it away. The agent told her he was sorry, but nothing from the bin could be saved. Mimi regretted not leaving them at home. She would know better next time she went on an airplane. Baba told Mimi not to worry. They would find wonderful lotions when they reached their destination in Africa. Mimi brushed back the tears from her eyes and managed a faint smile up at her dad.

Soon Mimi and Baba entered the huge airplane. Many people were already seated. As they buckled in, excitement flowed into every nook of Mimi's being. The huge engines came to life and they began to taxi down the long runway. Moments later the plane rose ever so gently into the air. Had she not been looking out the window, she might not have even realized it was happening. At last they were on their way. Baba told Mimi to sleep so she would be rested by the time they arrived in Africa. She had never been on such a huge airplane before and felt far too excited to sleep.

It had already been a tiring day, however, and before long Mimi was sound asleep. After resting for several hours Mimi sat up in her seat and announced to her dad that she needed to use the bathroom. Baba escorted her to the small bathroom in the center of the plane. It was a tiny room with just a toilet and a sink. Mimi stretched out her arms and her fingers touched both walls. She figured it was about the size of her tiny closet at home. She was amazed at how comfortable she felt on the plane. Her classmates had been apprehensive about how the long flight and jet lag might affect her. Mimi thought she was handling it very well. She returned to her seat and slept some more.

The next time Mimi opened her eyes it was morning. Soon breakfast was served. It consisted of scrambled eggs, toast, yogurt, apples, and orange juice. Mimi was very hungry and ate everything on her plate. Being fully rested, she decided to read her favorite book instead of watching a movie. Unfortunately, the book was missing from her red bag.

"Oh no! I've lost my favorite storybook," Mimi exclaimed as her eyes teared up.

Baba held her hand and said, "Cheer up, Mimi. Maybe someone who was very lonely found the book and is now enjoying it."

Her dad's calm voice and well-chosen words made Mimi feel a lot better, especially with the thought that some lonely person might be enjoying her book. Mimi decided she was going to enjoy her journey and safari no matter what else she lost.

Mimi selected another book. While reading, she fell asleep. She was awakened by someone announcing that it was lunchtime. After lunch, she played Monopoly with Baba. The journey to Africa seemed very long, but Baba promised that it would be well worth it. Mimi could not wait to see the animals. She had some questions about safaris. Baba explained that while on the safari they should see lots of animals in the wild and that they would need to be quiet not to scare them.

SWEET LEAF SAFARI

Mimi was woken from a deep sleep when the overhead lights were suddenly turned on. The pilot announced that the plane would be landing at Nairobi Airport in two hours. Mimi could hear everyone getting excited and gently putting away their books and games in their bags. Some people got up and went to the bathroom. Others were drinking water and eating light snacks.

Mimi and her dad joined other passengers in clapping as the plane came to a stop. It did not take long to get out of the plane. There were many people at the airport.

It was dark when they set down at the airport. Inside, they came upon a very tall man wearing a brown suit and a white shirt and walking through the crowd announcing, "Sweet Leaf Safari!"

Mimi's dad took her hand and they approached the man.

"We are here for the Sweet Leaf Safari," Baba said. "Are you the Sweet Leaf agent?"

The man smiled. Mimi was amazed at his sparkling, white teeth.

"Yes, I am your guide. My name is Kamau, but just call me Mr. K for short."

He then showed his company identification card to prove that he was their agent. Baba had spoken with Mr. K by phone several times before the trip and he had mentioned that he would be wearing a green tie, a light green shirt, and khaki pants. It was not unheard of for people to pose as tour agents at the airport, so it was important to make sure the man really was who he said he was. Baba asked Mr. K to verify their names and telephone number to make sure he was the real agent. Mr. K confirmed the information and complimented Baba for being so cautious. He then picked up their suitcases and moved them directly to the front of the customs line. There, Mr. K produced his identification card, and the customs agent began to clear their bags. The man clearly had the necessary connections that allowed the luggage to clear quickly.

Baba looked at his watch. It was 8:50 p.m. He became concerned that they might miss the bus. Mr. K assured them things would be fine because they would be taking a public bus commonly known as *matatu*. Mr. K also explained that *matatus* are not normal buses or taxis. They are inexpensive privately owned vehicles that anyone can ride as long the driver knows your destination and has agreed to take you there. For safety, Mr. K verified that the driver and his vehicle were licensed to do business as *matatu*. It is not unheard of for impostors to pose as *matatu* drivers in order to steal luggage from passengers. Some *matatus* can be very congested, but this one was very nice with spacious seating. Mr. K had asked the driver to wait close to the luggage area. The plan worked perfectly. The driver welcomed them and asked them to remain seated throughout the ride. When the *matatu* started moving, Mimi understood why they were not to move from their seats. The man behind them had a live chicken in his lap. The woman across the aisle had several bananas still attached to the stem lying at her feet. Next to her sat her two children quietly. Mimi asked Mr. K why there were so many people in the *matatu* at night. He explained that a lot of people had been working all day and were going home.

After a two-hour ride from the airport, the *matatu* let them off at Sweet Leaf Lodge. The lodge had a breathtaking view of Mount Kenya. It was ringed in green from the trees and foliage and capped in white snow. The mountain peak was topped with several small glaciers. The lodge was located amid a natural forest with birds singing melodies. They heard the wind blow softly. The atmosphere was beautiful and serene. The lodge entrance was surrounded by a bed of red, yellow, white, and purple flowers. To the left of the entrance were their bedrooms. The bedrooms had fireplaces and opened onto private balconies with unrivalled views of Mount Kenya.

At the entrance of the lodge there were several Maasai warriors standing here and there for security. Mimi had never seen a Maasai warrior before. Their clothing was unique. Each of them had a spear. When the wild animals strayed into the area surrounding the lodge the warriors made sure they did not get too close. Mimi and her dad were told that if the animals entered the lodge grounds they were to stay inside and remain quiet with all doors locked. They would be assigned a Maasai warrior every day who made sure they stayed within a safe area.

Sironka was the Maasai warrior assigned to them. He was friendly and quite talkative. He had many stories to tell. He told them how he had once been attacked by a lion and narrowly escaped death, and he had scars on his legs to prove it. As he recounted the incident it felt so real, it was like it occurred yesterday rather than fifteen years prior. It was after that encounter that Sironka decided he wanted to become a teacher. He was working at the lodge to save money for college tuition. He had saved enough for one year and was working on his second.

The lodge had steel doors and windows. Sironka assured them that it was very rare that animals tried to break into the lodge. Several years prior, an elephant had wandered to the front door of the lodge and tried to enter. Someone at the lodge set off sirens and the elephant ran away into the jungle. Sironka repeated that things like that did not occur often.

On the first day of the safari, Mimi and Baba woke up at 5 a.m. This was incredibly early for Mimi, but she was too excited to sleep longer. The sun was already bright, and from the cafeteria windows they could see Mount Kenya in the distance. Baba told Mimi that Mount Kenya was the second highest mountain in Africa, with its highest peak over 17,000 feet. At the tip of the mountain there was ice. She could see the blue, white, and brown reflections. The mountaintop appeared to kiss the blue sky. It was a magnificent view.

The cafeteria had lots to choose from. Baba told Mimi she could have what looked good but not to overdo it. The food was very tasty. Mimi particularly liked the mangoes, passion fruit, and papayas. She had never even seen a passion fruit before. The skin was wrinkled and tasted very sweet. It was the best fruit Mimi had ever eaten.

She asked Baba if they could take passion fruit seeds home with them so they could plant them in their backyard. Baba explained that fruits and seeds from other countries would not be allowed through customs back home. She would have to throw them away like her bottles of lotion. Mimi decided she was going to eat as much passion fruit as she could before leaving. She put three in her red bag for the day.

Mimi, Baba, and Mr. K drove to join the safari. It was a dusty, bumpy ride on the back seat of a Land Rover. Mimi did not even mind the bumps as she became more and more excited. The roads were narrow and not all kinds of cars could drive on them. She had to hold onto her seat tightly or she would be jostled from side to side and up and down. Mimi became nauseated and soon regretted eating so much food before the trip. She thought it would be a miracle if she made it through the day without being sick.

They soon came upon a sign that stated they were approaching the equator. Mimi had no idea what an equator is, but Mr. K explained that it is an imaginary line located at zero degrees latitude that circles the planet at its fattest point. She learned it is thousands of miles long and divides the planet Earth into the Northern and Southern Hemispheres (halves). She also learned that Mount Kenya lies south of the equator.

Still, she was not clear about what that means. Mr. K continued, explaining that the Northern Hemisphere includes all North America, the northern reaches of South America, about two-thirds of Africa, all of Asia excluding parts of Indonesia, and all of Europe. Baba added that the Southern Hemisphere includes most of South America, one-third of Africa, Antarctica, parts of Indonesia, and Australia. Mr. K had a map of the world and pointed out where the equator is. Mr. K did not know that Baba was a geography teacher and continued his geography lesson. Baba listened politely.

Mr. K went on to explain about the role African people think the equator plays in the African climate. Some believe that when the sun shines on your forehead at 2 p.m.

every day, it is a signal to think about drinking water. It is a useful reminder. Mr. K explained that when he was a little boy and would feel the sun on his forehead, he would get a drink of water for himself and would also check to make sure the cows had plenty to drink.

Along the way they came upon many splendidly dressed, very tall men carrying spears and arrows. Mr. K explained they were Maasai, like the warriors, and that they had cows that grazed all day in the grasslands. He told them a story of how he had once witnessed four Maasai warriors chase away a roaring lion that had wandered into their compound threatening the people and animals. The Maasai are known for being brave and never being intimidated by wild animals.

Mimi noticed one of the Maasai warriors with a beautiful bracelet. She immediately wanted one just like it. Baba inquired about it. A Maasai warrior pointed to a gathering of several women and children a short distance away alongside the road. He said they could buy a Maasai queen bracelet there. Her dad nodded and thanked the man. When they reached the women, Mimi and Baba were amazed at the variety of the beautiful handmade bracelets they were selling. First, Mimi picked up a white and black queen bracelet. Then she spotted a green, red, black, and white beaded bracelet that was just too beautiful to pass up.

She became more and more excited and moved onto necklaces. They were called *inkarewa* and were made of beads sewn onto a leather backing. They had thick, brightly colored rings with rectangular sections that rested on the chest. Long strands of beads and cowrie shells hung in the rectangular sections. The *inkarewa* are made by girls for their weddings, so it is important for the necklace to be as beautiful as possible. It was the practice pieces that were for sale. Each girl makes her own necklace, investing her very best skill in its design. They display the girl's talent and aesthetic understanding and are the source of great pride—a very personal object that contributes to her beauty. Mimi bought one of those necklaces for her mother. She knew she would really enjoy it.

There was also an area that displayed Maasai baskets. They came in many colors. Mimi's attention was drawn to one of the smaller ones. A Maasai woman explained that the basket was made of wire and beads and adorned with cowrie shells. The baskets had a lid with two handles. The basket Mimi liked most had a red and blue beaded strap. The baskets were made by girls, and each girl created her own design with alternating colors, arranged as a completely unique creation. The women used the baskets like handbags to carry their possessions when they went to the market. Mimi bought three of them for her friends.

Mr. K urged Mimi to purchase just one item at a time because there would be lots of opportunities to buy more gifts later. Mimi understood that would be a good idea but could not resist buying just two more multicolored bracelets with speckles in them.

Mimi and her dad moved on to the next area. They met women and men wearing clothing and jewelry that set them apart from the Maasai people. Mr. K knew a lot of people in this market and told Mimi and her dad it was important to learn about the people that were making and selling the jewelry. A woman appeared from behind a door made of colorful fabric and greeted them. The woman then gave them a quick lesson about the Samburu traditional dress, which consists of striking red cloth wrapped around like a skirt and secured near the waist with a white sash.

The Samburu people are well known for their beautiful handmade jewelry. Both men and women adorn themselves with a variety of colorful beaded necklaces, earrings, and bracelets. The Samburu also paint their faces using striking patterns to accentuate their facial features. They are a proud race of semi-nomadic people who still maintain their warrior culture.

As they drove back to the lodge for lunch, Mimi saw huts in the distance. These huts were made of special grass packed in mud. Mr. K explained that the huts were houses that protected the people from the rain and sun. The people slept in them at night.

Mimi really wanted to get a good look inside a hut, so Mr. K promised to take her to one after lunch. Lunch at the lodge was a delicious vegetarian dish made with beans, maize, greens, and bananas. It was served with chicken curry. Most people went for second helpings. Dessert consisted of mangoes, oranges, papayas, and passion fruit. Mimi ate two passion fruit and saved one for later. The papayas were delicious as well.

After lunch they had time for an hour-long nap. It was much needed after the long, tiring morning. The next tour would begin at three o'clock and end around seven. It was important to get back to the lodge before dark. Out in the wild, one of the warriors will stand guard at night, on the alert for animals roaming too close to where the people bedded down. If they see an animal coming their way, they wake everyone up and move on for the night. Sometimes they chase the smaller animals away by lighting a fire. On occasion, they even throw spears at the animals in defense.

In their villages, Maasai families live in clusters of houses called *enkang.* A thick "fence" of sharp thorn bushes encircles the group of huts and acts as a protective barrier. Mimi learned that each *enkang* includes several small huts made from branches and pasted with fresh cow dung which bake hard under the hot sun. Mr. K explained that the *enkang* protects the Maasai and their cattle at night from wild animals and rival ethnic groups who might try to steal them under cover of darkness.

Maasai huts are very small, usually with two rooms and ceilings not high enough to allow Baba or Mr. K to stand upright. The huts are also very dark, with only a small doorway and tiny hole in the roof. Mr. K explained that this hole serves as a chimney as well as a light source. The Maasai people love nature and spend the majority of their time outdoors. The kids play and eat outside all day and return to their hut at night to sleep. Mimi thought this sounded like a simple, uncomplicated life!

Mimi noticed a long, fragile-looking flask in one corner of the room. It was decorated in bright colors and interesting designs. Mr. K explained that the flask was a large gourd full of fresh and curdled milk, a popular part of the Maasai diet.

It became obvious that red is a favorite color of the Maasai. Most people were dressed in bright red wraps. While they were there, the Maasai began dancing in unison in a unique up-and-down manner. Mr. K explained that the Maasai dance is driven by jumping, voice, and the shaking of jewels, but no actual musical instruments. One tall man led the group while other men danced with their spears. Soon it was the women's turn. They also danced in unison, using the same up-and-down motions. They shook their colorful necklaces, which provided an interesting sound and rhythm. Mimi was amazed at how excited the people became when dancing. They had make-up—of a sort—on their faces and feet. It was their way of looking well groomed.

Mimi asked Mr. K why the people seemed so happy that day. He reported that there was a wedding and the whole village had come to witness the ceremony. The dance went on for about an hour. It was the longest continuous dance Mimi had ever witnessed. Another full day over, they returned to the lodge.

For Mimi, the next day started early—at six in the morning. They wanted plenty of time to see the animals which lived a bit further from the lodge. Learning from her experience the previous day, Mimi decided to have a light breakfast. Mimi had a delicious deep-fried bread known as *mandazi.* This pastry tasted like a donut, but with cinnamon and cardamom flavors. Mimi went for seconds.

Mr. K said it was going to be another very bumpy ride. The three of them were soon on their way along the dusty road. The first animals they saw were very tall.

"Wait! I see an animal in the distance!" Mimi screamed with excitement. "What is it?"

"It is a giraffe," said Baba. "It is the tallest of all land animals. It is even taller than many of the trees."

Mr. K continued, "Giraffes' front legs are longer than their hind legs. Their necks are very long, sometimes longer than two meters. They sleep for only about five hours a day and feed from the trees, grass, shrubs, and fruits. The name 'giraffe' comes from the Arab word *Xirapha*, meaning *the one who walks very fast*."

Mr. K explained that the giraffes are one of the largest, strongest, yet most peaceful animals on Earth. However, in a fight a giraffe can kick a lion to death. A large male giraffe may consume a hundred pounds of food in a day. A giraffe can go for several days without water. They often live for about twenty-five years.

"Look at the giraffes necking," Baba tells Mimi. "When giraffes rub their heads and necks together like that it is called necking. Giraffes do this necking to show which animal is more dominant—which is the leader."

Mimi realized for the first time that giraffes are one of the most beautiful animals on Earth. As they came closer, she could see that the giraffe in front of them was huge. It walked gracefully and with confidence, staying close to the trees. It seemed to be unaware of its hidden enemies, the human beings.

Mr. K told Mimi that giraffes have disappeared from many areas over the years because men hunt them for their tails, hides, and meat. Mr. K added that the giraffe tails are used for charms and thread. It became clear to Mimi that men sometimes do senseless things like destroying beautiful, peaceful animals for very selfish reasons.

Baba asked Mr. K to drive on down the road to where there were fewer trees. They came upon many different animals that were relaxing, some in the sun and some in the shade. Mimi thought it seemed like they were having recess. They were careful not to make noise that might startle or disturb them.

There were just a few giraffes there, near the trees. Mr. K drove close enough to see them in some detail. At the top of a giraffe's long neck sits a strangely shaped head. Its eyes are situated on the sides of its head, which gives it a wide view from side to side so it can detect enemy predators at a great distance. Baba explained that the long neck allows the giraffe to feed on the fresh new leaves at the tops of very tall trees. That way they can easily share range areas with animals that feed from the plants at ground level. Mimi wanted to get still closer to the giraffes, but Mr. K warned that giraffes neither make any noise themselves nor like to hear noise close by.

Mimi decided to just sit back and take it all in. It was a beautiful scene. The giraffes with their oddly shaped spots stood tall and proud. In the background were blue skies and white clouds. The horizon was broken here and there by a few lonely trees. The sun was bright and the air was clear. Mimi could have stayed there for a very long time.

Baba pointed out a herd of antelopes not too far away. Mimi later learned antelopes have extremely developed senses which help them detect predators while they still have time to escape. Antelopes are known for their running speed, which can reach over forty miles per hour. As herbivores they eat grass, seeds, and leaves.

Mr. K reminded them that they needed to move on. The next animals that came into view were elephants. Mimi had seen pictures of elephants, but seeing one in person was a whole different experience. The first elephant they came upon was even bigger than the giraffes they had just seen. Mimi felt quite tiny compared to the massive animal. From what she had seen up to that point, the elephant clearly was the king. For such a large animal, Mimi thought it moved with grace and confidence that surpassed all the other animals. The elephant was simply huge!

Up close like that, Mimi realized the animal could step on their car and totally crush it into scrap metal. She suddenly became uneasy. There seemed to be nothing protecting them from the power of the elephant. She was not sure she would be able to move fast enough to escape if it turned on them. Her hands trembled. She moved to hide behind her dad as they stared at the elephant through the open top of the vehicle. Her dad held her hand and reassured her that all was going to be fine.

The elephants went about their business, walking and feeding as if the people were not even there. They seemed to have no concern about their presence. Elephants are herbivores and eat only plants, and they live in harmony with many wild animals. Mimi noticed that the giraffes, zebras and antelopes in the distance seemed to feed without worrying about the presence of the elephant. Clearly, they had worked out some kind of agreement to leave each other alone.

Mimi later learned that although the giraffes are the tallest, the elephants are the largest living land animals on earth. Some elephants have lived to be eighty or more years old. They can weigh over 10,000 kilograms (over 22,000 pounds), which would be the equivalent of 100 to 130 human adults. A female elephant is pregnant for twenty-two months (almost two years) before giving birth to a baby. A newborn elephant can weigh 100 kilograms (220 pounds).

Lions are just about the only animal that can kill an elephant, and the feat requires a good deal of luck and much difficulty on the lion's part. A lion would never attack an elephant when it is with its herd. Elephants are one of the animals that come to each other's rescue when threatened.

The main danger to elephants is people. The elephant, because of its size, cannot hide easily from human hunters. The main reason people kill elephants is to get ivory from their tusks. The thought that someone would kill such a peaceful and beautiful animal for ivory to make jewelry made Mimi very sad.

Mr. K said that elephants have been used to help humans with labor for many decades. Their great size and strength make tasks such as uprooting trees, moving logs, and crushing unwanted objects relatively easy for them. They also provide transportation, as people can ride on their backs. Mimi realized that the elephant's size and power do not amount to much next to the humans' powerful guns. She wondered why the police do not arrest the people who are harming the animals. Mr. K said there are not enough policemen in the game reserves and forests. Most of the time, the hunted animals are not found by the police until it is too late.

It was difficult for Mimi to understand why the bad people get away with killing animals. Mr. K said that one day, if enough people hear about what is going on, they will work together to stop it. Mimi asked Baba what they could do to help. Baba suggested that they should tell as many people as they could about the terrible war being waged against the wild animals, especially the elephants and several other endangered species.

Mr. K suggested they move on to a different area which would offer a better view of the elephants. Watching them interacting with each other, Mimi discovered that the huge animals were very gentle. They eased their heads against each other and kept a close eye on the babies that frisked in between and around the adults' huge legs. It was like a family in which aunts and uncles and brothers and sisters all lived together quite happily.

Surrounding one of the elephant's feet were a few birds picking at seeds stuck in its hoof. The elephant clearly knew they were there but was careful not to step on any of them. It was as if they were friends and the elephant was enjoying spending time with them. The birds showed no concern that the huge elephant might pose a threat.

Mimi thought that humans should learn to live like the elephants. She decided that humans, although more technologically advanced, with cars, phones, guns, books, and such, had no business harming such magnificent animals. She thought elephants and the birds had many important lessons to teach human beings. Baba and Mr. K smiled at her and nodded when Mimi told them she would always remember the elephant and the birds and how well they got along.

Mr. K explained to Baba and Mimi the first rule of thumb in a safari: Never get out of the car unless you are informed by your guide that you are in a safe observation area. They soon came to one such area and could pin-step out of the car, though they had to stay within a few meters' distance.

Suddenly, an elephant uprooted some plants with its tusks. Baba explained that the tusks were the long pointed "hands" on each side of the trunk which the elephant used for digging, ripping bark off of trees, resting a heavy trunk, and as weapons. Up close, Mimi felt ridiculously small compared with the elephant. For the first time in her life she realized her dad could probably not protect her if the huge animal decided to charge towards them. Something came over her and she started running back to the car as fast as her ten-year-old legs could carry her.

Baba and Mr. K were surprised when they realized how frightened of the big animal Mimi had become. They both walked calmly in her direction. Her dad reassured her, saying, "It's OK, Mimi. You can stop now."

Mimi sat on a rock and waited for her dad and Mr. K. The elephant continued eating leaves. As far as it was concerned, nothing had happened.

They agreed to take a break. They walked to the dusty vehicle and made their way back to the lodge.

They all relaxed with passion fruit juice and fresh pieces of pineapple. It was sweet and delicious. The server had brought an entire pineapple to their table and sliced it into pieces. She said the juice was very refreshing on a hot afternoon and made a healthy dessert. The server related local lore that told how the sugar from the fruit would sweeten their souls and help them to become incredibly happy by the time they left. The local people often recommended the sweet pineapple to guests who looked worried or were not smiling.

Mimi thought her math teacher would certainly benefit from the fruit, because she rarely smiled and looked sad most of the time. Her mood was so unpleasant that Mimi and her classmates were often hesitant to ask her questions. Mimi figured that if she brought a sample of the fruit back to her, it just might give her as much warmth and happiness as the server promised. It was certainly worth a try.

The server invited Mimi to watch her peel the pineapple. Her name was Mama Sarai, which meant Sarai's mother. She explained that in the local culture it was considered polite to address a woman in that manner.

She first placed the pineapple on a large cutting board and slowly peeled the leaves from top to bottom. She then meticulously removed each rough edge with a wooden tool. According to Mama Sarai, the woman who served the pineapple must very carefully remove the rough edges before serving. If they were not removed, the pineapple would be less sweet. She then opened a big drawer, removed a good-sized knife, and carefully cut the pineapple horizontally. She said the fruit had a big "bone" in the middle and was loaded with a lot of good stuff. Once she cut the fruit into small rounded pieces, Mama Sarai placed a big wooden toothpick in the middle of each piece and instructed them to hold the toothpick without touching the fruit. The fruit was to be eaten in a circular manner, with no juice dripping on the floor. The last part to be eaten was the bone in the middle. Mimi thought the fruits in Africa tasted better than any she'd eaten at home. Baba said perhaps it was the type of soil these fruit trees grew on that made the fruits so sweet.

Baba, Mimi, M. K, and a driver got into a big safari car. Different parks have different rules for the type of safari vehicles allowed inside. The road to the safari was not too rough, although the car got stuck in the mud a few times.

Next Mimi saw a huge animal in the distance, different from any other she had seen so far. As they got closer, it became apparent that the animal had two large horns: one in the middle of its big face and another at the top of its head. What made the sight more amazing was, this animal had relatively short legs and a short tail.

Mimi's dad held her hand, knowing she was getting a little scared and excited at the same time. He pointed to the animal and said, "Dear, this is my favorite animal. It is called a rhinoceros, but many people call it a rhino." He walked around to get different views of the rhino. Soon, another rhino appeared from behind the bushes. Mr. K said Mimi and her dad needed to get back in the car and drive slowly towards the animals. Mr. K went on to explain that they were looking at two white rhinos.

"As far as I can see these rhinos are grey in color. Why are they called white rhinos?" Mimi asked her dad.

He said color had nothing to do with their names. In fact, white rhinos were not white and black rhinos were not black. Mr. K went on to add that white rhino's name came from an African word *wyd*, which means "wide" and describes its mouth. People later misinterpreted the *wyd* as "white," and that is how the grey-colored rhino ended up with the name white rhino.

Mr. K asked Mimi, "Did you know a group of rhinos is called a crash?"

"Wow, that is a surprising name!" she said.

Her dad started singing a song that he and Mimi both liked. Mimi joined in, and they intuitively knew they had to add one more sentence to it now.

"*We call a group of fish a school, hello, hello.*

We call a group of alligators a congregation, hello, hello.

We call a group of frogs an army, hello, hello.

Yes, here comes a group of penguins called a rookery, hello, hello.

What about a group of hyenas? Yes, call them a clan, hello, hello.

We call a group of lions a pride, hello, hello.

We now know we call a group of rhinos a crash, hello, hello!"

They all chuckled and sang the song a few more times.

Mimi's dad turned to her and asked her to pay close attention to the rhino's horn and skin. On its back were small birds comfortably standing, picking at its skin and watching the surroundings.

Mr. K explained that rhinos have made friends with birds known as oxpeckers. In Swahili, the oxpecker is referred to as *askari wa kifaru,* which means "the rhino's guard." These birds act as a rhino's guard by creating a commotion when they sense danger. The commotion warns the rhino so it can react to the threat in time. On the other hand, the oxpecker eats ticks and other parasites that live on the rhino's skin. The relationship between the rhino and the oxpecker is a symbiotic one.

Baba explained that there are five species of rhinoceros and they can grow to weigh over 2,200 pounds! There are two species of rhinos found in Africa: the black rhino and the larger white rhino. Sadly, poachers used to kill the rhino for its horn, which was supposed to be used as a type of traditional medicine though it was not proven to be effective. Rhinos were hunted nearly to extinction.

Not too far away from the two white rhinos was a heavy-set animal with stocky legs, a large head with horns, large ears, and a short neck. To the right was an entire group of these animals lying down, and they appeared to be looking towards Mimi and her dad. Mr. K said these were called *nyati,* or African buffalo. He told the other two to get in the car right away because the buffalos were unpredictable animals.

Mimi was reminded of the story that her mum told her about kids missing school because a couple of buffalos were roaming through their village.

"Oh my," she thought, "this must be the animal that Mum told me was nicknamed *Black Death*." Her heart started beating extremely fast, and she held on to her dad's hand as tightly as she could. Once they got inside the car, Mr. K drove away slowly. He asked Mimi and her dad to close their windows and to be quiet so as not to startle the animals. Once they left the area, Mr. K confirmed that African buffalo are dangerous animals that kill several humans every year. That was why they were not allowed to get too close to them. Sadly, Mr. K added, the African buffalo is hunted by man for meat and trophies.

After they had snacked and relaxed, it was time to return to the animals. Mr. K said it was the ideal time of day to see baboons. It took well over an hour to get back to the safari.

The yellow baboons were amazing and nothing like Mimi expected. One with slim hands and legs sat staring at them while he munched on a large piece of fruit. He looked like he was very much enjoying listening to their conversation.

Mr. K explained that a yellow baboon can live up to thirty years. Baboons are known to be very social animals—much like humans—and usually live and travel in groups often consisting of two hundred or more. Several larger males usually take the lead while other males follow behind, protecting the females and the young by surrounding them. Mr. K said it was alright to leave fruit behind for them since they would surely find it and eat it. Mimi was happy to leave her sweet mango behind for them. It wasn't long before one of the younger baboons picked up the mango, sat down, and began to enjoy the sweet treat. The baboon held the mango in its hands almost the same way a human being would. Mimi understood why the local people said the baboons were both skilled and clever animals.

Mr. K asked Mimi if she would like living in close quarters with the same group of people for the rest of her life, like baboons do with their groups. Mimi could not imagine a lifestyle in which she would never be more than a few feet away from everyone she knew. In physical education class the students had to walk for one hour in groups of twenty, and even that was uncomfortable for her. The thought of living in such close proximity with her classmates for the rest of her life was not a happy one. She wondered how the baboons felt about it. She thought it must be similar to the way a human might spend their entire life among family, friends, and local community—the difference being, baboons did not live in separate houses.

It dawned on Mimi how selfish humans are—how they often drive animals away so they can have more space for themselves. She questioned her dad about it.

"It's not fair. Why do animals have to live in such a small amount of space while we humans continue to take more and more space?"

Baba explained that unfortunately unless the rest of the world realizes what is going on, the poor animals might be pushed out of their homes entirely. It had already happened in parts of South America.

Mimi was curious and wanted to know if there were any organizations or groups of people speaking up for the animals. Baba said that there were and when they got home, he would help her find the names of some of them. In the meantime, she needed to do what she could to help her classmates understand the sad situation. They, in turn, could help make the grown-ups aware. Mimi realized that her trip to Africa was already changing her life. She had envisioned a safari as merely fun and entertaining, but now she came to see how it was going to change her views about wildlife forever and add a grand new purpose to her life.

Mr. K explained that some baboons were already becoming extinct and said that there were groups of people dedicated to preserving them. It was just not happening fast enough. He had some brochures back at the lodge that Mimi could read and take home.

At that moment three young baboons appeared with their mother. They swung from tree to tree as if they had no worries or fears. They played together much like human children would. Mimi chuckled as she watched. Deep in her heart, however, she understood what they could not know—that someday their lives would very likely be made both uncomfortable and difficult by thoughtless humans who wanted to cut down the trees and plant crops or build new cities. Baba sensed her growing sadness and suggested they move on to another area.

Their next stop was less than a mile down the road. There were about two hundred and fifty baboons there. Many were swinging from tree to tree picking and eating ripe bananas. Mimi was amazed that they knew how to peel a banana. She could tell they were really enjoying their treats and decided that being a baboon must have its perks. She also liked bananas.

That was the way Mimi's safari trip ended—with memories of happy baboons playing in the treetops and enjoying what seemed to be an endless supply of bananas. After a restful last night of the safari, Baba woke her at 8 a.m. and reminded her that they needed to pack their bags for the trip home. Mimi reflected on the wonderful time she had spent with her dad. She had lots of pictures and gifts to share with her friends and family. Most important, however, were the priceless, wonder-filled memories that she would carry with her forever. Although Mimi was only ten years old, she was determined to work hard to make a difference in the way humans treat wild animals.